Journey to Pluto

Adapted by Jordan D. Brown
Based on the screenplay
"From Pluto with Love"
written by Craig Bartlett

Ready-to-Read

Simon Spotlight
New York   London   Toronto   Sydney   New Delhi

SIMON SPOTLIGHT
An imprint of Simon & Schuster Children's Publishing Division
1230 Avenue of the Americas, New York, New York 10020
This Simon Spotlight edition April 2019
© Copyright 2019 Jet Propulsion, LLC. Ready Jet Go! is a registered trademark of Jet Propulsion, LLC.
"Dear Little Frozen Pluto" © 2018. Lyrics by Craig Bartlett and Jim Lang.
All rights reserved, including the right of reproduction in whole or in part in any form.
SIMON SPOTLIGHT, READY-TO-READ, and colophon are registered trademarks of Simon & Schuster, Inc.
For information about special discounts for bulk purchases, please contact Simon & Schuster Special Sales
at 1-866-506-1949 or business@simonandschuster.com.
Manufactured in the United States of America 0319 LAK
2 4 6 8 10 9 7 5 3 1
ISBN 978-1-5344-3056-3 (hc)
ISBN 978-1-5344-3055-6 (pbk)
ISBN 978-1-5344-3057-0 (eBook)

Mindy was flying through space
when she saw a friend.
"Hi, Pluto!" said Mindy.
"How are you?"
"I'm fine," replied Pluto, smiling.
"Are you sad that you used to be
called a planet and you're not
anymore?" asked Mindy.

"No, I like being a dwarf planet,"
Pluto replied.
"Small is special, right?"
"You bet!" answered Mindy.
"I'm also special because I'm
super cold," said Pluto. "I live
far, far away from the hot sun."

"How cold are you?" Mindy asked.
"I don't know," answered Sydney.
Mindy wasn't really in space.
She was in Jet's backyard
on Earth with her friends.
Sydney was telling her a story,
and pretending to be Pluto.

Mindy really wanted to know
just how cold Pluto is.
"Is it too cold for humans?"
she asked.
"Yes, Pluto is way too cold
for humans," answered Sean.

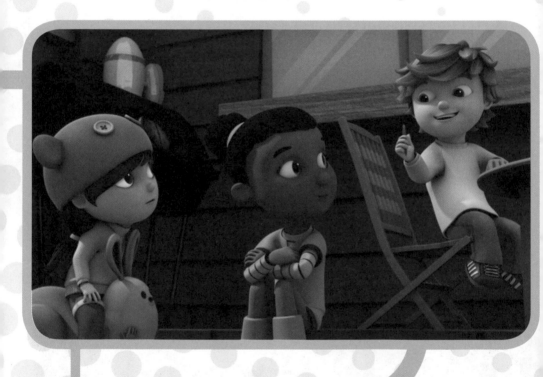

"Do you think Pluto is colder than the coldest place on Earth?" Jet asked.

Sean said he wasn't sure.

He did know that the coldest place on Earth is Antarctica.

It's covered in snow and ice, even in summer!

Sean pulled up photos of Pluto
on his tablet.
"These pictures were taken
by New Horizons," he said.

"What's that?" Mindy asked.
Sean explained that New Horizons
is a spacecraft that can fly fifty times
faster than a jet plane.
Even at that speed, it took
New Horizons nine years to fly from
Earth to Pluto.

"Nine years!" said Mindy. "That means Pluto is really, really far away."

Jet spoke up. "My mom can fly to Pluto in our flying saucer in just nine minutes."

"That's because your family's saucer is from Bortron 7!" Sean said, laughing.

Jet and his parents are space aliens visiting Earth from a planet in another galaxy.

Mindy looked at the picture of Pluto and made a discovery.
"Look at that big heart! I love it!

Then Mindy had an idea.

"What if we made a card for Pluto?"
Mindy asked her friends.
"Great idea!" Jet responded.
"Can your mom drive us in the
flying saucer out to Pluto
to deliver our card?"
Mindy asked Jet.
"Yes!" Jet answered.

Sean wasn't so sure.
"Is this trip really necessary?"
he asked.
"Pluto is really, really far!"

Mindy looked at Sean
with huge, sad eyes.
"Please!" she pleaded.

"Oh, okay," said Sean.
Mindy jumped for joy.
"Thanks! Let's start making that
card for Pluto!"

So Mindy and the others got paper,
crayons, and scissors to make
a beautiful card for Pluto.
Then they had to decide what to say
on their card.

Sunspot played his guitar
while Mindy began to sing,
"Dear little frozen Pluto,
we live so far apart!"

Sydney added the next part.
"I love your little frozen ways,
and your big, white icy heart!"

Jet's mom arrived in her saucer
and told the kids to hop in.
"I wish I was big enough to go,"
Mindy said, handing the card to Jet.
Jet gave Mindy his special phone.
"Here! When we get to Pluto,
you can watch and talk to us."

Everyone fastened their seat belts.
Jet's mom stepped on the pedal,
and the saucer zoomed into the air.
"Ready, Jet, Go!" the kids shouted.

Soon the ship entered outer space.
Sean was still a little worried.
"Are we going to freeze on Pluto?
I didn't bring my long underwear."
Jet's mom told him it would be okay.
"This saucer can take the cold,
and our space suits can, too."

During the trip, the saucer's computer told everyone more about Pluto. "Everything on Pluto is frozen. Even the air there freezes into snow."

When they arrived on Pluto, Mindy showed up on the screen. "Wow!" said the kids as the saucer flew over the big, icy heart.

"Pluto is so cold
and so pretty!" Mindy said.

Seconds later Jet's mother landed
the saucer on Pluto.
"Let's get out there
and skate around!" Jet shouted.
"Maybe I'll stay inside," said Sean,
feeling scared.

"We'll all go together, Sean,"
Sydney said.
Sean started to feel a little better.
"Let's deliver our card," he said.
He left the saucer
with the rest of the team.

When the group stepped onto Pluto,
the first thing they noticed
was how dark it was
and there was ice everywhere.

They were excited to see
cold volcanoes that spit out ice.

They had a Pluto party.
They skated and sang.
And they made sure to give
Pluto the card they had made.
And even though she was far away
back on Earth, Mindy's heart felt
almost as big as Pluto's.

Read on to learn some fun facts about Pluto, Antarctica, and space! And how to create your own card to give to someone you love!

Facts About Pluto

- Pluto was discovered in 1930 by Clyde Tombaugh (say: TOM-bah). The white heart on Pluto, called Tombaugh Regio, is named after him.
- Pluto got its name from Venetia Burney, an eleven-year-old girl from Oxford, England, who suggested it be named after the Roman god of the underworld.

- Scientists changed Pluto's classification from planet to dwarf planet in 2006.
- Pluto has five moons.
- It takes Pluto almost 248 years to complete its orbit around the sun. It only takes the Earth one year!

Space Exploration

- The New Horizons spacecraft was launched by NASA (National Aeronautics and Space Administration) on January 19, 2006.

- New Horizons was the first NASA spacecraft to reach Pluto. Its mission was to better understand this dwarf planet.

- New Horizons did not reach Pluto until July 14, 2015—that's almost ten years after its launch! It sent back lots of pictures of the dwarf planet!

Our Solar System

- Our solar system is made up of one star, eight planets, and countless smaller bodies such as dwarf planets, moons, comets, and asteroids.
- In order of distance from the sun, the eight planets in our solar system are: Mercury, Venus, Earth, Mars, Jupiter, Saturn, Uranus, and Neptune. Pluto is a dwarf planet past Neptune.
- Our solar system is in the Milky Way Galaxy. It takes our solar system 230 million years to complete one orbit around the galactic center of the Milky Way.

Facts About Antarctica

- Antarctica (say: ant-ARK-tick-ah) is the southernmost continent on Earth.
- The name "Antarctica" comes from a Greek word meaning "opposite to the north."
- Around 90 percent of all the ice on Earth is in Antarctica.
- Even though Antarctica is covered in ice, it's actually a desert! It only gets two inches of rain (in the form of snow) per year—that's less rain than in the Sahara Desert in Africa!

- There are only two seasons in Antarctica—summer and winter. In the summertime, the sun doesn't set for six months and in the wintertime, the sun doesn't rise for six months.

- Because of the cold, no one lives permanently in Antarctica. Scientists and other workers only stay temporarily to do research.

- There are more than one hundred volcanoes in Antarctica, but they're mostly all covered by ice.

Is there someone or something special in your life? Make them a space-themed card to tell them how much you care!

1. Take a piece of paper and draw a picture of Earth, Pluto, the moon, some stars, or whatever you like. Just keep a space theme in mind. Use crayons, pencils, paint, or whatever you like drawing with the most. Leave room at the top of your drawing to write your note.

2. After you've finished drawing your picture, write a note to the person you want to give your card to. You can include a fun space phrase like "You're out of this world!", "I love you to Pluto and back," or "You are a shining star!" Can you think of other fun, space-themed greetings?

3. Don't forget to include your name so the person getting the card knows whom it is from.